ONE REASON WHY NOT TO

ONE REASON WHY NOT TO

ANNANYA KAKKAR

pencil

ISBN 978-93-5458-307-0
© ANNANYA KAKKAR 2021
Published in India 2021 by Pencil

A brand of
One Point Six Technologies Pvt. Ltd.
123, Building J2, Shram Seva Premises,
Wadala Truck Terminal, Wadala (E)
Mumbai 400037, Maharashtra, INDIA
E connect@thepencilapp.com
W www.thepencilapp.com

DISCLAIMER: *This is a work of fiction. Names, characters, places, events and incidents are the products of the author's imagination. The opinions expressed in this book do not seek to reflect the views of the Publisher.*

Author biography

It is my immense pleasure to introduce you to my first ever novel "one reason why not to".
Writing this novel has taken a lot of love and courage and there are so many people I owe thanks to for allowing me to share it with the world.

I owe huge gratitude to my family and friends for encouraging me and supporting me in every way . I thanks all the readers for acknowledging my hard work and getting up related with my characters.
Life" is such a wide umbrella; a word that covers many, many things, and everyone's experience of it is different.
And sometimes we also need to get put back together again; to be reminded of the ways we can get through this, how we have overcome, and how, despite it all, life gives us hope.

CONTENTS

Introduction

ONE REASON WHY NOT TO

Need to know basis

People are usually born once but hey who are these people who are born twice, god am I a vampire? A ghost? Or a freaking soul surrendering itself in search of the pure me? So if I ask you who are you? What you'll say probably you'll indicate me with your name and what if I ask you again after knowing that you're Tanya a young girl. What you'll answer?

That you're from a rich family graduated from Delhi University with a degree in Economics Honours from SRCC struggled to become next millionaire. But indeed my question wasn't for knowing what you are doing with your life and what you did but I just asked who you are? We casually answer such statements not realizing who we really are. But the irony is that if I ask this same question to you will you be able to answer this question correctly accommodate to the answer I'm looking forward for?

My mind is wandering. Is it the ego that continues to say-"it's me"? We human being have practically discovered everything, but we have not discovered ourselves. We go under the seas and oceans to discover who we truly are and what lies on the bed of ocean floors. We only touch the tip of our physical and emotional self. And instead of realizing that everything is a miracle, we are trying to prove that nothing is a miracle. Therefore the world's biggest joke is who are we? Where we'll go? What we are going to do? When we'll die? Why are we here and what we must do? Doesn't it seems so strange that we don't give importance to our lives understanding the true reason why do we exist, we have been so busy with this world proving ourselves the best but do we exactly know who are we? We are so much highlighted with the modern era of life spent on possessions. When will humanity wake up to the truth to realize the down fall, the chaotic chaos, the drama and move from a life of illusions to truly living? How can I be something that is constantly changing?

So here am I Soumya, a girl born twice once on 18th August 1999 and then again on 11th May 2017. What happened why I woke up again half dead? Am I a zombie struggling? Well maybe a zombie with some depressed mind and soul. What happened that a young girl was forced to born twice? The family is wealthy, living a charmed life. But every family member has a secret, some dark side of their own. Reminding myself that my family loves me is a part of my daily routine now. Am I lying to myself? Can even people love me? Will they accept me? Will my family accept me? Plenty of questions to be answered. Shall I stop complaining? Will my life be a little self or less destructive?

Is the world ending in my glittering eyes where my dreams were high headed to live to be a self wondering soul, what the world needs from me why I'm still alive actually barely alive just breathing.

Rohan is a student of a well-known and a prestigious college "The Delhi school of economics" where his dad has been a member of the charitable trust of the college, with a well settled business in the economic sector. With all the riches in his life, Rohan starts his first year with a fully known personality as the son of the richest person of the college. Entering the college with all the lavishes and leaving with them has been a daily routine of his life. Having a crush over a classmate Alisha, Rohan is always intended to seep through his own world to exclaim his feelings to himself. With all the family quarrels taking place, he tries to get rid of them and henceforth brushes himself into his own thoughts of madness, love, affection and self-pity. He hence proclaims that he is a person whom no one understands but still keeps looking for his proclaimed love instead of living his life on his father's money. Would he be able to make through all of this to find his soul-mate or would he end up in a tragic end?

CHAPTER ONE

SAUMYA

All clocks stuck at three. Water washes over my skin so strongly that it feels as if I am in the flow of a river rather than a rain shower, one that leaves me standing yet lets me know that it is here to stay for a while. And so the only thing to do is to keep walking, to accept it as easily as the air I am breathing, to see it run over the earth beneath my soft soles. The icy Grey sky restlessly grumbled and the thick blackened clouds were dragged down by the heavy rain which it held in its delicate frame. The clouds which struggled to withstand the burden of the weight which the rain held, soon gave in. The rain poured down over the city with a roar. The sound of emptiness was disrupted by the loud gregarious boom of thunder. The cold icy rain pierced her pale and wet skin. She ran across the slippery path, her posture weakened by the weight of her soaked clothes. The quality of darkness shifted in the sky but the rain kept pouring. The harsh rain obliterated the crystal reflection of the sky and turned it into the disorientated chaos. Rendering my thought to what happened an hour ago to me has broken me entirely once again. Coming back home from my classes I found my house all empty just with 3 workers working and my driver. Those were the days we were not allowed to have cell phone before clearing our 12th standard boards.

"Dear, ma'am left a letter for you they'll be back soon"
Kamlesh, member of the working staff exclaimed.
I was way too happy reading it and knowing my family is
out of town and will return back late at night.
The letter wrote;

"Dear Soumya,
We are sorry we couldn't take you with us, we were in a
hurry,
hope you'll understand. Don't be a silly girl wasting your
time,
do some left over chores, clean my room and cook
yourself a meal
don't bother the working staff as they have other plenty
of work to be completed.
We'll be back by midnight."

"Hush, at least I got my me time. Lets bang the floor
Soumya, it's time for fun and of course to do the chores
with the same scenario", I exclaimed.

The weather was just as pleasing as my mood and as
wonderful as to sip coffee on rooftop, I used to love rain
before the incident happened to me, after this I was barely
alive to feel this type of love from the weather within

myself. I tried finishing off with my work, I cleansed my parents room with high banging music over lifting my veins and cherishing every moment dancing over the floor, enjoying the very popular music cheap thrills.

'Till hit the dance floor
Hit the dance floor
I got all I need
No I ain't got cash
I ain't got cash
But...'

What an amazing afternoon it was I fully enjoyed with my hips and every other body part dancing to the beats of the song, I got all I need yeyeyeye'

Suddenly the song changed and so my life with such a wrecked and awful incident,

'You were the shadow to my light
Did you feel us
Another start
You fade away..'

The driver entered my parents' room while I saw the change in my playlist. he at first didn't uttered a single framed sentence nor a word explaining his need to see me. He just kept glaring at me with his horrible eye sight. I was about to rush out of my room and then he suddenly pushed me away into the restroom and those dirty hands started rushing all over my body. It felt pain within, within my tiny glittering eyes which were young enough to see what was correct and wrong but a young girl couldn't help herself landing into a wrecked piece of her life.

The hands rushed all over trying to pull me closer but I managed to pull him back rendering myself to the in disciplinary thoughts, emotions and mixed feelings. I just wanted to run away from this world where humans were treated badly. These shallow waters, never met what I needed, I'm letting go a deeper dive eternal silence of the sea I'm breathing, Alive.

A heavy thunder storm started, I cried, I shouted but no one heard my voices, screaming within myself my utmost silence, my emotions I was all stuck to them at once.

'The monsters running wild inside of me
I'm faded
I'm faded
So lost'

No, no, no, what should I do now my brave heart aggressively shouted within me. He tried to wrap my father's pajamas, which were hung on the wall to my mouth so I could stop shouting and no one could find out about this and what all happened but somehow I managed to cut his hand with my sharp teeth and I pushed him away leaving his hand hurt and ran out of the room. I just ran to the kitchen where rest of the staff members were gossiping and working causally.

'What was I supposed to do now? Am I supposed to tell them what the driver did to me?', my inner voice needed answers to all my stupid questions.

No I can't tell this to anybody what happened to me. I just

can't! My parents won't believe me and they'll point out my mistake to this even. What to do now?

Running off to THE nearby park was the only option available. I didn't want to face anybody at the current point of time I was broken into pieces, plenty of small pieces which seems impossible to be picked up and kept together I just lost all my hopes, all my confidence striving to achieve in my life with such an awful incident that took place to me.

Running off the streets crying and screaming in this heavy thunderstorm and rain poring making me feel more lonely and depressed.

'The person that he made me
the person I've become
and I've been tryna fill all of this empty
but, fuck, I'm still so empty'
Now the baggage in my heart is so dark and deep carrying this heavy load of emptiness,' If I could break my DNA to pieces to get rid of all my demons if I could cleanse my soul then I could fill the world with all my problems but, shit, that wouldn't solve them.

So, I'm left here alone.'

I roar and storm away from this worldly affairs. I'm done. I yell, struggling to break free from this grasp. Suddenly I'm picked up and swung over. It wasn't too late realizing I came back home and I failed miserably in my attempts to escape. I saw him coming near me and all other staff was still busy working ignoring and realizing I too exist in the place of nowhere.

'Let me go!' I screamed again, punching him in the back as he carries me up the stairs and into my bedroom, where he drops me unceremoniously on the bed.

"Sleep this off," he simply says.

Who the hell he thinks he is? I rush towards the door, but he quickly slips out and shuts the door. I get to the door a split second later and yank on it. It's locked. That bastard has locked me in.

"So are you kidnapping me now? In my own fucking house? You're adding that to your resume as a shitty, emotionless, bastard human. You can't keep me here locked!"

My outburst is futile. I can hear the play-by-play of the bulls' game echoing up the stairs, and I'm certain it was a master plan of all the workers working out here and has now turned up the volume on our stupid-ass giant radio in order to drown me out. I sit on the floor screaming and crying until I can't cry anymore, until I'm too tired to do anything but sleep.

I adjust my eyes as I wake up realizing my eyes still wet, my head pounding, no longer on the floor but in my bed with the covers over me.

The day dawned crisp and clear. The sun poured through my window. Another day had dawned, bringing with it new hopes and aspirations. The light of dawn seeped into my room. I rubbed my bleary eyes and walked to the window. There was a pearly glow in the sky. The first rays of sunlight lit up my room. The dawn chorus of melodic birdsong drifted in. The rising sun cast a rosy hue across the morning sky. Golden fingers of sunlight lit up the scene. The just-risen sun shone softly on the city streets, bringing with it a flurry of early-morning activity. I move back inside. The bedroom is now unlocked. I open it only to find that all lights are turned on and if the family has returned back to the basic. He's gone, which doesn't surprise me. Being inside alone feels suffocating. I walk back onto the terrace.

The loneliest time of my life has begun. His touch awakened every nerve in my body. For so long, I couldn't breathe. I laugh at my naivete and wipe a few tears from my cheeks. Dammit. I promised I wouldn't cry over this instance anymore, holy mother I can't narrate this to anyone about what all happened they'll judge me uncertainly and of course my family will be ashamed of me and won't accept me either. But another promise broken by me? I try to not to care so much, but I'm not fooling anybody. It's me who's suffering.

The sky was an expanse of sapphire blue, dotted with feathery white clouds as the radiant rays of the sun shone brightly in the azure blue sky. Stuck over with my over thinking in my head trying to act normal and move on to the fact that I'm being suffered alone a voice stabled me from back;

'Is there anything you want us to know?' Mum-ma said.

'So nice, seeing you back, Mum-ma. How have you been? All good?' I asked covering up my tears and emotions.

'Dear I don't have plenty of time to answer your silly questions. You gotta tell me what you did last night to the driver and other staff members that they want to leave? I don't need any explanations got ya? Answer me right away!'

Me trying to figure out what has been the scenario, and what the family was told about the past day incident, making up my mind to tell the truth to mum-ma but tears were all way down on my cheeks, eyes glittering out of tears.

'Look I never came up here for your mellow drama and things, also stop crying you need to accept what you did and you'll be the one suffering and from now on will be doing all the chores of the house. I don't need your fucking explanation now so shut the fuck up get downstairs have your breakfast and start with your work.' she said.
'But... Mum-ma... I wanted to talk to you about.. .'
'Stop all this I don't have much time to waste I gotta go work, bye. And I need all the work to be finished within an hour!' she said.
"Okay!"

CHAPTER TWO

Rohan

As the morning sun peeps through the curtains, hitting the eyes of the open world, with a shiny mist on my face I rise upon my bed. With the bottle of juice pouring into the crystal white glass I got served with my morning snack. Every riches of my life paving the way from my dad's business into the alluring apartment I live in.

Being In the first year of my college made me a pretty prominent student, not only just because of my money, or was it because of that? Well who cares when everything in life goes as subtle and smooth with the business hitting the peaks and college making me a timid but a so called personality I had my limits to be utilized in the most precise-full way possible.

College life had been a big transition from my school life. Going through a lot of changes made me a person as dumb in the school ages to as famous in my college days. The transition to college was so sudden that even I couldn't control the fact to put out with everything my dad provided me with.
Entering the college with a sparkling white Mercedes, I was now in a place full of unfamiliar faces where I

definitely needed to mingle in. Both did it teach me to socialize and form opinions of my own but also paved ways for me to enter into a different world all together. As they say in college, "students learn their free will and they go on to become more confident and composed." I still had the replica of my childhood focusing to conquer my life.

My mom and dad had been going through a traumatizing situation since the past five years. By achieving the riches of life even I think my dad didn't gave some of his demanded time to my mother which made each other to give up upon my daily activities. I had been through a phase of life which I never would feel any kid would actually try going through.

I've always wanted to mix up with the people at the back seat but to protect the very own rich attitude, I had to keep up with the so called buddies.

As days passed dad started to include me into his awful business which I had never even supposed of entering. With my good ties with a college friend Alisha, I sometimes felt of making her my girlfriend. But who wants a buffed up life with no fun in it.

I open my eyes and my dream fades in the early-morning light. What the hell was that about? I grasp at the fragments as they recede, but fail to catch any of them. Dismissing it, like I do most mornings, I climb out of bed and find some newly laundered sweats in my walk-in closet. Outside, a leaden sky promises rain, and I'm not in the mood to be rained on during my run today. I head upstairs to my gym, switch on the TV for the morning business news, and step onto the treadmill. My thoughts stray to the day. I've nothing but meetings, though I'm seeing my personal trainer later for a workout at my office. Maybe I should call Alisha? Yeah maybe. We can do dinner later this week. I stop the treadmill, breathless, and head down to the shower to start another monotonous day.

The bonding with Alisha had been making me crave to talk to her the whole day. Even my pals made me think about dating her for a while to see if it works out between us.

Well… I am not much of a date person. And that is for several pragmatic reasons.

But if a date has to be perfect, there are three elements that need to be perfect - person, place and shared activity.

There should be shared chemistry with the person. Dates get super awkward when people try to please each other by doing things that they wouldn't normally do. You have to click and it should come naturally.

The choice of place is a matter of personal taste. For me I don't like dates at crowded places or popular eateries or theme parks or stadiums, even cinema and long drives … Any place where you cannot talk or you have to focus on something else. The place should be beautiful, peaceful and not compel you to engage into anything other than spend time with each other.

The last piece is the shared activity. You can talk which can be interesting to both parties. I don't like eating because I am a clumsy eater and a food lover. So, coffee seems a better idea than parties. Walking by the side of a safe, less crowded and beautiful road by sunset is a lovely idea. A carnival with none scary rides is a good idea.

But never mind I was definitely not the one asking her out. It makes me feel like a horrible person. For a lot of reasons, sometimes talking to your parents about your dating life might not be constructive. Maybe they're just going to lecture you, lay down a bunch of rules, or ask too many invasive questions. For some people this can also include dealing with homophobia, racism, or other kinds of bigotry. Especially in those cases, in addition to reaching out for help, you can also keep in mind that your parents don't need to know everything (especially if knowing everything will put you in harm's way) and even after everything going inside my family. I am definitely not giving it a shot to tell them about Alisha.

Often the stars and the moon amazes me, they make me realize the world is so much larger than the Jonas brothers latest album, but I wouldn't mind dancing on the epic Bollywood songs with someone under the moon light under the stars. Everytime I look above I stretch my arms to reach the moon. To grab it and hold it as close to my heart wherever I go as a lucky charm tied on my neck to feel complete, but couldn't. Instead I talk to the moon, it teaches me how to love all my phases like it does, and how it's okay to feel incomplete sometimes.

People often claim to know me, yet they keep me back on the shelf like the fancy book they think they know just by reading the preview. I am not a puzzle, not for everyone to solve. I've spent months trying to fix myself, to place the pieces where everyone said they should be, but then I realized that it was supposed to be this way, scattered and still beautiful. Rather I wouldn't mind if you call me an art for not everything has to make perfect sense, and neither do I.

Winters have never been my favorite, though they have their own romantic way of making the frost feel like a perfect mood, but no matter how much we try some things aren't just made for us, so I wait for summers, only for it to come back. Soaking up the sun, although at times getting a heat stroke but then sitting in front of the cooler reminds me of my childhood, the tiny water droplets with the cool breeze passing through my hair, reminds me how carefree we used to be. Where goodbyes meant meeting until tomorrow, and when school bags used to be heavier than hearts, I digress.

I am not lost, but rather a new resident in the place I call home. And I am also a wanderer, I'm on a lookout to find myself with everywhere I go I build myself. I am an old school, I still listen to mix-tapes for my different moods and wouldn't mind sharing it with you. But, only if you promise to sit with me through all my phases, under the moon.

After all the future lies into the mystery of my words. And to that there's a lot of fun in going through the epitome of life at the stages when they're meant to. Such a phase reminds me of some wise words.

"You can never hold onto something for eternity and the good things always end too fast.

The candle that was lit at the night has melted along with my heart.

Sometimes I can hear you in my cupboard. Sometimes I can see you next to me.

Sometimes I try to grab onto nothing, maybe the ghost of

you.

Maybe I will one day move on, maybe I'll meet another. Maybe I will find it once more. That feeling from within me has escaped."

You can always stand there watching me. I'd hold onto the cliff, about to go crush the waves. Grappling to pull my weight up and ponder through the shimmering eyes of the ocean. The solemn eyes of the ocean wave at me as I leave my soul to depart through its arms. It's then I know, I am the cliffhanger which no one understands.

CHAPTER THREE

Saumya

Moped the floor, cleansed the garden, watered the plants, did the dishes, terrace painted and sat with a sigh of relief, suddenly a message popped up;
"Hey Saumya, Congratulations !" , Alisha Didi texted; my school senior.
And plenty of congratulation messages flooded my inbox, what the fish! Dammit! Are the results out? Holy crap!
I rushed to my room in search of my laptop to check upon my 12th standard results. I was praying to get good grades so as to get admission in Alisha's college.
What next? Where is my admit card? I searched everywhere then remembered my mother gave that paper to my younger brother's in case they ran out of papers making jet plains out of my important sheets. The next thing that I did was to call up Arshima to get my roll No.
Arshima: "Hey Saumya! Congratulations buddy you rocked it girl. You made us proud. I'm so glad we are friends. So now what are your plans for college, umm SRCC or..."
Me: "Hey Arshi, you seem way too excited. Can I get my roll no. I gotta check my results, I've been busy never knowing the results were out"
Arshima: "Ya sure, but you scored highest in Economics, English and Political Science. You are our school topper.

Teacher's were trying to reach out for you maybe they tried contacting your parents but I guess they never answered."

Me: "I don't know about that. Can you please send me..."

Arshima: "Yes I've the screenshot of your result I just mailed you, check once."

Me: "Thank you!"

Arshima: "You alright?"

Me: "Bye"

Emotions have by far always been one of the most difficult thing for me to express. I've always had a hard time being comfortable with tears or even showing my happiness. Throughout my battle with depression, I often thought happiness and joy were for others, but not for me. I thought happiness might be something I never feel. I think I am not worthy of happiness, or joy, or anything positive. I can't say I come by emotions easily to this day, but I am starting to express them more and more. But mainly the negatives. I have gotten much more comfortable with tears running down my face (though I still try to fight it), and I'm afraid to say when I'm happy or excited about something. But one thing I never thought would happen, is that I'd cry tears of joy just because of a pretty good day. I scored 97% in 12th boards, it was way too difficult for me to express what I was feeling. Past one month was difficult for me to breathe entirely changing what I feel physically or emotionally. I wasn't complaining this time but wasn't happy anymore.

I stepped out of my room with a print of my result searching out for Mum-ma. She was busy with a call I waited for next few hours to get her available for me. After two certain hours I could make a move to tell her that my results are out and also that I scored highest in my school. Seeing my report card she looked at me, seems not so happy and cheering but making a face to get rid of it. I completely got distorted with my feeling, the way I was happy left again. The feeling of achieving something left again. My heart broke all over again. The only thing she said was "Oh! Results out! Failing this time? Or an average student like every time?

Sometimes I try to find a solution so that I don't have to be sad. But with deep thinking I get to know without sadness the recipe of life is incomplete. To give a taste to the recipe, I need to put all the emotions in the plate of life. The energy put in suppressing the emotions bounce back with the equal reaction. The sorrow I try to escape from will come back and hurt me more. But the only way I can find my happiness was now to text back my batch mates ignoring all this daily shit and try not to focus on what's bad for my health. But I was happy to imagine myself in the Delhi School of Economics. I know the feeling of being in a place you'd rather not be. Anyways, it's sometimes better not to think about it.

I glance at my watch. It's four thirty in the morning and my bed is calling. I hope my parents are asleep, they usually have a complaint me getting up late in the morning by 7 a.m. I take a deep breath and remind myself I need this college. I've grown to hate the whole situation. First the obligatory awkward conversation with mum and my over thinking I feel completely dead. I sneak away to the terrace. It's my favourite place; I get to be alone with my loneliness. When the wind blows the right way and the lights of the street sparkle in the night, I feel free. They remind me why I'm still here struggling to make my life better. This may be my lucky day. I could stand here for hours, just looking out over the streets and the dark clouds just like my life. I glance at my watch noticing it turning day it's been five fifteen in the morning. I decided to head back to my room before anyone catches me here. I'm afraid to look up. I can hear my heartbeat pounding in my ears. When I work up the courage to finally fall asleep.

One Month Later

'Soumya got her admission in the Delhi school of economics which was her dream college, now her eyes just craved for respect from the society.'

Soumya: "Mum-ma, tomorrow is my first day for college."

Mum-ma: "Okay! Wake up early and do the chores and then go."

Soumya: "Alright!

Surprisingly, Soumya shed no tears for her dead emotions. She did not frown, she did not smile. It was as if she did not care at all. Its six in the morning Soumya gets up early trying to finish all her daily chores and gets ready for a new journey for life.

It was A very bright sunny day. The day was 1st of August 2018. The very First day of my college. After lot Of hustle bustle, wait, lengthy formalities And sincere hard efforts I had managed to get admission in that college. I was feeling nervous, at the same time. That strange feeling we all go through but can't explain exactly.

Finally the day comes. I wore my favorite Tee with denims as I want to look cool And Casual. Nothing Over. Then I reached my college. As I entered the premises I inquired for my class. It was on the first floor. There were lot of students with their parents as well. I went to my class and sat on the second bench. There were few other people sitting there as well. This is really very awkward feeling sitting there not knowing anyone. There was still time for classes to commence so I started staring at the beautiful walls painted. Here comes a girl who seems too talkative in nature she sat next to me and started questioning me about how I was and so on. I was quite and intense both at the same time and didn't bother to answer her silly questions perfectly. But there was something how we clicked together it was way too beautiful to me. She has such a vibe which is so pure and for the first time I felt like talking to someone after the incident. It felt so good to me. We started talking about other students who entered into the premises with grand brands and expensive cars; Mercedes, Jaguar, Audi was so normal even we could point out some expensive sport cars. The next thing we did was exchanged our numbers and our first class got canceled so we headed towards the canteen area. Tanu was way too excited to see rich crazy brats shining all over with Mercedes. She always wanted a cute crush for herself I guess, which I could make out with her nonstop talks.

"Soumya, see him! He's so cute! Ain't he?" Tanu said looking at me with her shinny blue eyes.

Next moment Tanu went crazy stating; "I like him

Like him too

He my man

He my boo

He my type

He so cute

I want him

And I want him too"

Such a blessing she's to me. She tried to keep me happy and excited about the start of our new college journey. She wasn't aware of the fact that what I was suffering from but she got a hint that I wasn't alright. We then decided to head back home we were just at the parking lot and I met Alisha, my school senior. And suddenly Tanu notice a random cute guy starting at Alisha and me. We talked for a while and then I insisted Tanu if I could drop her back home. She denied but the next moment she saw me with the grand jaguar she said yes! Hahahahah!

We enjoyed that afternoon and I dropped her back home and even I headed back knowing plenty of work piled up for me back there. Meanwhile Tanu told me about that Mercedes cute guy but I wasn't sure how to react to it so I felt it causally.

My clock Stucked four thirty in the evening, a young girl tired returning back home I dropped my car keys at the entrance, rushed to my room changed my clothes and got back to my work.

After a good walk a way from home and plenty of gossips with Tanu I felt a little self in past few months.

But in this universe can even a girl like me deserves to be happy?

CHAPTER FOUR

Rohan

All eyes turned to her.

"Look," Sahil says, pointing towards a beautiful girl, as she entered the college canteen area along with her friend.

We were sitting around the dark wood table in the canteen, eating chilly potatoes. Those spicy potatoes tasted more spicy with the look that girl gave and her smile adding more spice to our food. Something is really up with her. Dammit. This is process. I smile and am rewarded with her answering shy smile. Meanwhile, Alisha entered the scene and that certainly made my day. She wore pink skinny tube top with black pencil skirt and white snickers. Her long brown hair pulled up till her waist added more beauty on her. She's a perfect example of beauty but the girl next to her is too cute giving her tough competition. Alisha knew that girl.

"Rohan, see Alisha! That girl is her known, come on dude lets adjust ourselves within their conversation, maybe we could make up with them", Sahil said running towards them and of course me following him as usual.

"Good morning, Alisha." Sahil says.

"Morning."Alisha broadly smiled at us.

"So how have you been all these vacations? No texts, no

calls?" Sahil making up stories for some forced conversation with Alisha, trying to know the juniors indeed!

"Can we guys just shift for a coffee or tea maybe?" Alisha moved towards the table adjusted her skirt, tying her hair into a messy bun.

"I never imagined Sahil, we would be able to make up till here. My goodness!" I whispered into Sahil's ears. We started giggling like younger girls now unaware of the fact that the girls were noticing us.

So let me introduce, this is Sahil, my batchmate and of course the flirtatious one, this is Rohan he's my batchmate as well the prince charming of our batch and such a shy kid he is. So boys she is Soumya my school junior and a sweetheart with a perfect smile, and she's Tanu Soumya's friend a nice and talkative girl, hahahah." Alisha said as she introduced us all together.

Meanwhile, I thought am I prince charming? Alisha introduced me as a shy person too. As Sahil made a gesture to me to start a conversation.

"So nice meeting you guys, hope you'll like the college and the faculty too. If you find any difficulty or anything just let me or probably let us know." I said with my eyes on the table, feeling shy and jumbling with words as my eyes couldn't resist all beautiful girls in front of me and all at the same time somehow feeling that Alisha's words defining me as a shy personality was true.

"You're going?" Tanu asked abruptly.

"Shall I? if you guys want to continue and if we are disturbing you..." I asked.

"No, that's not the point. We actually made a plan for an outing maybe exploring nice places near the campus. Will you?..." Tanu's voice disappearing as she asked us out.

Sahil: "I'm in for all such stuff and in for sure when I get to have such amazing cuties as my side chicks, smirks."

Alisha: "Sahil, you such a jerk."

Tanu: "Well kinda impressive, smirks too."

Alisha: "Where are we heading guys?"

Me: "Shall we decide that own our way?"

Soumya: "Guys you carry on but I have to return back home after my lectures. It's just some guests coming over for dinner and I have to be there before time. So sorry you guys enjoy."

Tanu: "Come on Soumya! It will be fun and I promise you that you'll be back home soon and on time."

Sahil: "I guess you hate me, Soumya. Am I that bad? Alisha, how about your opinion in this?"

Alisha: "Shut up Sahil! Join in Soumya or you'll regret later."

Me: "Soumya if you want to come join us we promise we'll be back on time."

Soumya: "Alright!"

We all decided to head towards a great adventure and everyone decided to eat as we all were hungry not minding the spicy chilly potatoes anymore. I insisted everyone to join me in my car and we begun with our journey. The clock said twelve in the afternoon, Soumya seems a bit nervous as I drove, everybody started gossiping about the college and the faculty. It felt amazing how we just clicked in not even knowing each other perfectly, the day seems impossible to me slightly.

As everyone was excited to exchange vibes Sahil was unstoppable as he continued to flirt with three of them where Alisha ignoring my champ and Soumya! Soumya sat next to me she wasn't interested to Sahil's useless talks and kept quite noticing other folks from outside the window. She was a simple girl, less talkative and, and I don't know, It never happened to me before but this time my focus automatically shifted from Alisha to Soumya. I was craving to see her pretty smile all over again, knowing that she barely smiles. Her's is a hard earned smile and also one in a billion! I made a gesture asking where to go and Soumya pointed out towards a strange dhabba to have her lunch. It was way too profound to let us there but that place seems interesting too. I parked my car near to it and the place stated 'Chache Di Hatti' it was a popular place for Delhi students, we sat outside near the roadside where Soumya wanted us to sit, but Soumya was way too busy looking to some poor children at one corner playing with their own catastrophe, Soumya had so much to say within. I wanted her to see smile all over again even if it's meaningless. She should know that her smile is so pure that it could make someone's day. That smile is the prettiest thing I've seen in a while, for it extends to your eyes and deep into your soul. Her smile is such a gentle touch, the honesty that is a purity, it portray ones childhood innocence that is so vibrant and free. She contains the whole universe in her eyes and her smile makes that priceless. Not flaunting but when I saw her smiling for the first time my heart flattered and my mouth was wide, it was a heaven on earth, but what is making her helpless for herself. I was completely stuck over Soumya, lately noticing Tanu and Sahil chilling on the other hand Alisha secretly blushing talking over a call while Sahil and Tanu placed our order. But seeing Soumya was so comforting that I could do that task like for hours. Soumya was busy in her own way arguing within herself with some badass rubbish thoughts, winning arguments with herself in some other world.

It turned almost one and the order was placed to us; spicy, exotic flavour, succulent, moreish, perfumed, wafting aroma, air saturated with spicy perfume, mouth-watering, salivating in anticipation, drooling uncontrollably, watching the food as if we hadn't eaten for weeks or months. It seems so delicious without wasting any more time we all grabbed our thallis and almost frowned for more, still Saumya was stuck over the poor children.

After some gossips where no such gossip took place eventually, Sahil and Tanu were busy all together flirting, Alisha busy with her call, Saumya dreaming in her own world and then there's me busy looking up for Soumya and building my stories within.

I still wait for the day when I can show the small beauties of life to someone, but there are no fools like me in this vast world. Perhaps they exist, yet they must be distant, enjoying the same sky with other eyes yet the same thought. I whistle with the birds that awaken from their sleep in the trees, letting my vision be painted white, yellow, and red.

I checked my watch again, it says two and Soumya gently said "please drop me back!" We all knew it was time to head back but we all enjoyed, it was fun connecting with people you never know about what happens next. I drove back to college admiring Soumya's silence and her sufferings. She has a lot to say, her damn eyes says all about her. We reached college I dropped everyone but I secretly wanted to talk to Soumya. What if we never met again? Plenty of questions running in my head, calming my soul to act wisely. I wanted to follow Soumya so that I

could talk to her but I wasn't that brave!
May be better luck next time!

CHAPTER FIVE

Saumya

One week later*

From the pool of shadow that bathes my feet and nothing else, I know it is midday. But in this late fall the sun has lost its intensity, I can step out without fear of burning. The streets would have been deserted at this time of day, but now the street vendors carry on selling and there is no shortage of customers. Reminding myself about the harsh reality that it's time to head back to work and prepare dinner for the family I had to leave my terrace comfort and be back to kitchen. Somehow the situation ain't that critical but this damn over thinking and jumping over conclusions with some false thought kills up more. And with no doubt I can say we girls develop so much within, that our over thinking at a certain point of time starts ruling our daily thoughts and actions. Some days I feel so bad about being a girl so as to face this disrupted way of thinking and reacting.

It's seven in the evening and I need to prepare dinner and do the dishes, Mum-ma busy with her work and daddy will return late night. My brothers are cuties no doubt but then the feeling of jealousy never fades away, why from the universe I get such negative vibes. It's not just about today but I am craving for my parents love for past ten years now! While I was preparing dinner which was supposed to be 'rajma-chawal' I decided to make it a special dinner for my family adding more fun to serve them with some hot mouth watering 'Gulab jamuns'. I never felt like not doing too much for my family or getting a thought even how they treat me but at last they are my family.

My brothers were the luckiest and also the prince charming of my family as they were BOYS and somehow patriarchy super rules. Not over thinking about any past incidents which made me realize that my parents don't love me, I finished cooking. The clock said nine thirty now, I beautifully placed the dinner in the dining hall with fresh table clothes and handles to look more pleasing and soothing. Everyone arrived and sat on their favourite seats ignoring all the special arrangements I made for them. Everything started being toxic again. Nobody seems excited to know what's for dinner, everyone busy with their cellphones avoiding conversations, suddenly daddy entering the whole scene and pointing out to what I was wearing, I was shabbily dressed he made a gesture to my mum and she pore more spice to the wordings and exclaimed "Don't ruin our reputation in your college and at home even, get some proper clothes for thyself you idiot! Don't wear such worn out clothes maintain your standards and ours too. So please before entering into college premises get yourself a look, girl."

That was so weird pointing out my clothes I love wearing baggy clothes, dammit. Anyhow, I need to obey their orders. So meanwhile I decided to go shopping the next morning and to attend lecture a little late. It all seems so mad to me that I wasn't hungry anymore avoiding everything I did the dishes and returned back to my room.

My phone showed 27 missed calls from Tanu, she probably needed me or something else. I didn't bother to call her back or felt like even leaving a message. I was still using that J Samsung cellphone in the world full of IOS. Never mind. They have a thing that they always want themselves to be superior in eyes of others so they want me to be well dressed, maintaining high standards regardless of my emotions and feelings.

Another thing that kept me thinking is Rohan, He was handsome from the depth of his eyes to the gentle expressions of his voice. He was handsome from his generous opinions to the touch of his hand upon my own. I loved the way his voice quickened when he sparkled. He had the kind of face that stopped you in your tracks. I guess he must get used to that, the sudden pause in a person's natural expression when they looked his way followed by overcompensating with a nonchalant gaze and a weak smile. Of course the blush that accompanied it was a dead give-away. It didn't help that he was so modest with it, it made the girls fall for him all the more. Despite all the opportunity that came his way I guess he was a one-woman-man who prized genuineness and thoughtful conversation above lipstick and high-heels. He was handsome alright, but inside he was beautiful. And then I realized it was two in the morning and casually I decided to lean myself over my unicorn and sleep as another tough day is waiting for me tomorrow, deep inside wanting to see him again, which I haven't in past few days but I made up my mind to visit him tomorrow.

The next morning, was ultimately more depressing after noticing a grand new iphone kept aside with a note on it labeled as don't take that old crap to college anymore, switch your sim into this gadget. Sometimes I feel it's all what matters are your high standards, your luxury and the amount of money you earn in today's era. As everyone is more likely to fake high standards with social media and stuff, upbringing themselves in the rat race which is neither too important, ones goal in life should be to prove themselves to their oneself not to the outer world, we are so much surrounded by the energy of what will the society say that we render our own thoughts, emotions and feelings. Such a useless rat race! Everything that's bright isn't heaven and everything that's dark isn't hell. Anyways, I finished with my daily chores and got ready for my college and shopping as well, switched my sim into my new phone. Today was a new day to me no more negativity followed my thoughts this morning, deep inside knowing I was excited to see and meet Rohan.

This morning I was feeling myself by getting ready. I was already late and it Stucked ten in the morning I rushed towards CP I somehow tried to arrange contacts with the manager at h&m, they let me in while I found CP almost dead, the crowd one could see at night wasn't available and although that wasn't highly excepted. I handpicked few clothes and managed to wear a skinny top all black with high waist white jeans and my belts added more confidence to my outfit. How can I forget to mention my footwear which were way too adorable, all white boats with four inches heels. I myself looked adorable. I was feeling myself after couple of months. I tied my hair into a messy bun with glares on top of it. I looked perfect. I wanted to be at my college the next minute wanting to see everyone's reaction. I drove my car towards college and parked at the starting of the parking lot. It was almost the first break I called up Tanu to know where she was. I came out of the car and all eyes stopped on me, everybody for a second went like 'stop and stared like a sculpture.' Never mind, my eyes were looking for just one .I managed to spot Sahil and there she was, Tanu. Seeing them together I clicked like something's fishy why they are so close to each other and remembering those late night multiple calls. What were those calls about and for?

I entered their scene while Sahil holds Tanu's hand and they two were laughing. The moment they saw me they were shocked to see the real me they got lost with their mouth wide open. I just smiled a little and then Tanu asked is today your birthday or something special why you're so beautifully dressed. I casually smiled not willing to answer her question, happy enough to know they liked my dressing sense.

"Oh hey, Sahil! How you doing haven't heard a lot from you after that day. Am I that boring?" I asked him as I tried to sound more of a savage queen, such a dumb bitch I'm, trying to figure out where Rohan has been all these days.

"You look so damn pretty babe. And where is your prince charming, haan?" Sahil said, not making a correct statement if Rohan finds me cute, anyways I'm not making a move I decided. I kept on thinking why in this universe I even tried to be happy. I just wanted to give up with the thought that even I can be back to normal, which was way too difficult that it seems to be. I wanted to go back home, put my baggy clothes on and wanted to cry on some corner in my room.

Leaving all such thoughts I decided to attend my lecture, asked Tanu if she was joining me into it. She made a gesture telling she was busy at that moment and I patiently headed towards my classroom. I was on my way to the classroom, not feeling much confident now and almost looked like I was forced to dress-up like this, moving quietly, tears rolling down to my cheeks with my head down.

"Hey, is that you Soumya?" a sparkling voice was heard suddenly.

I turned around hiding my tears, managing to wipe them away quickly. so here he was, Rohan. But till this point of time my confidence and my excitement to see him eroded.

I didn't wish to ignore him but it happened so sudden that It felt rude to me as well. I just got away with Rohan stating "I'm late for my lecture, cya." and to be honest I said it abruptly. All my mixed emotions resulted for some bad reaction for the one I was excited the most from the very beginning of the day.

CHAPTER SIX

Rohan

"Let the fun begin, trip to Spiti Valley", as I read the notice board Sahil came running to me shouting my name in the corridor and such a crap he is that he got so excited that he banged his head on the notice board.
I simply asked "what's next now?"
Sahil: "What do you mean by what's next ain't we going there buddy? Rohan see last year we had our internals and this time we ain't having any such excuse and I don't want built up stories for the same now. We are going and that's final!"
Thinking about this I made a statement stating "Ain't this going to be boring? Like we don't have many friends and just the two of us?"
Sahil: "Did I say that only we two? No, we all are coming, I mean we all five! Well I don't know about Alisha's new boy friend but..."
Oh so now Alisha got a boy friend, woah! I wasn't even interested more for Alisha now and suddenly I got covered up thinking if Soumya was also joining us for real. It would be fun like accompanied with such heavenly good friends and of course the beauty of all the time, Soumya!
I was so lost in my own deep thoughts that I forgot that Sahil was still talking to me. The next moment I realize

that Sahil was still talking Tanu and Alisha entered the scene, talking nonstop as I kept wondering where Soumya was, continuously staring at them. The next minute Tanu just waved her hand in front of me, so closer to me to realize that they were standing next to me. I was so lost with my thoughts. Alisha looking up at me figuring out if I was okay, Tanu ignoring everything hugged Sahil and says "Good Morning, babe." Alisha and I were shocked realizing they both got together, and none of them even bothered to tell us about the same. Alisha enchantingly describes her new relationship with a guy who works at Tata Power DDL as a manager. She tells us about him and their relationship, me ignoring all the shit and suddenly I asked "where's Soumya?" nobody knowing where she was and Tanu explained her bad mood swings from past one month and the next moment I decided to talk to her patiently, I texted her a simple "Hey!" Obviously this was a very difficult and courageous task for me to deal with, what if she keeps me on seen or maybe even worse directly blocking me either. Multiple thoughts started running in my head till she texts me back and that took her almost the whole evening till then I headed back home after attending few lectures of mine making a deal with my new group that we all are going for this one week vacation to Spiti Valley. But deep inside I knew I was way too worried for Saumya and what has happened to her I wanted to make her feel safe and happy. Her smile is so precious that I never wanted to let her pretty smile fade away. So to avoid such stressful thoughts I played fifa and for the first time it felt so boring to me, I wanted to drive somewhere far away but at the same time I wasn't sure what she was suffering with. So I texted her again "You there?", still no response I acted so desperate and texted her twice, maybe she never wanted to answer my text or something like that. I decided I won't text her multiple times now if she wants to answer she will. Now I headed towards rooftop to have some fresh air, grazing at those beautiful stars and not able to avoid my thoughts. A message popped up, I prayed it should be Soumya. And yes my prayers were answered it was Soumya's message.

Soumya: "Hey, Rohan!"

All excited I replied with enthusiasm, "Hey, how have you been? I was worried is everything alright?"

Typing…

Typing…

Last seen one minute ago…

How can I be such a jerk, just over flowed my emotions and ended up with just hey! Five minutes later there was a big paragraph, I was shocked.

Soumya: "No I'm not alright, I have been through a lot and I don't know if I'll be surviving through all this or just be dead the next moment. I have just failed in my life putting up a facade in front of my darkness I don't deserve any kind of happiness in my life now I just need peace and wish to be dead"

I was shocked to hear this all from her to be honest and wanted to know what exactly was in her mind. "Soumya! Calm down. I'm here for you always, will you please tell me what's going on if you feel safe and secure sharing your thoughts. I would love to help you to overcome this."

Soumya: "I am really sorry to bother you Rohan with my silly texts and I don't even know why I'm telling all this to you, hope this stays between us two!"

"Chill Soumya you can completely trust me and it's not

silly, I was seriously worried about you and now I want to know what's all happening with you." I was worried knowing all this thinking if she wanted to cry over my shoulder and needed me.

"Rohan, Thank you so much for being here for me and I seriously don't want to bother you midnight." Soumya cried.

"Okay, now I'm not hearing anything else get yourself a cup of milk as I'm sure you haven't had your dinner and go back to sleep. Tomorrow I'll pick you up from college at ten thirty sharp and we are going for a drive and we need to talk. And don't worry it's just you and me. And this stays a secret!" I was so nervous about what she says next, she left me on read and me praying she shows up tomorrow morning.

It was really difficult for me swallowing that she's in trouble and none of us was aware about the same. I felt so shameful that she wasn't able to share her problems with us. But why did she mention to be dead and in peace, has something really worse happened to her. All these thoughts jumbled inside my head and I wasn't able to get a proper sleep.

"Rohan, get up kid! Aren't you getting late for your lecture at the university. It's almost ten dear, get up!" Mums voice realized me I was late. I rushed, showered quickly and drove to reach college as early as possible. I never wanted her to wait only if she shows up. I texted her where she was and I'll be waiting for her at the main entrance. She seen zoned me again. I was broken into pieces, I had put on my favourite black t-shirt with black jeans and white sketchers wholeheartedly excited to see her but I could see my dream vanishing but I kept waiting for her for next half hour, no text message stating I'll be there or not.

Suddenly I noticed her coming her face so pale and eyes all swollen, lips not moisturized, wearing baggy clothes unaware of the fact that everybody is noticing her. I came out of my car opened door for her and everyone started with their dumb conversations. I simply ignored all this and moreover I'm worried about her. At first I never wanted to initiate a toxic conversation so I simply said, "let's go for coffee." she simply nodded while noticing random people on street.

Listening to classical music, I thought it might be soothing, but it's really irritating and has no proper tune. I'm absolutely frozen. I couldn't believe she had so much to say. We thought we'd all go to Cineplex for the day.

I simply looked at her and went on.

CHAPTER SEVEN

Saumya

Rohan cheered me up with a cup of coffee and I felt safe with him. My blood chills. So much has happened in the last three weeks- who am I kidding, the last three months that I feel my feet haven't touched the ground. And now here I'm with the most sensible, polite and charming guy, Rohan.

Without wasting time I made a statement "Sorry I'm bothering you, but what happened to me wasn't easy to me and till date my sufferings are painful and I can't trust anyone."

Rohan kept staring at me half lost in his own thoughts and unmindful of what's coming next to him. He didn't utter a word and I wanted to continue the story without making any other excuse not to.

"This journey was hard for me but I gotta spell this out to you, not realizing why I'm sharing this to you but I guess this vibe is connecting us." I said jumbling and hustling with my words.

The very next minute I started narrating him the whole story about the driver and my parents, how I suffered during all these days, it felt almost he completely lost his interest in me knowing these past issues of mine. I don't know what's happening next.

It was two in the afternoon and I finished dictating him all my life story till date and afterwards we ran out of awkward silence. This silence was healthy no doubt but I was worried will he leave me too? Still over thinking ruling my actions and mind not allowing me to look at him even, disrupted with my thoughts that he might go. The silence continued for next ten minutes and I made up my mind that people enter in our life for some lesson and to leave as well, the one who comes eventually leave someday. Also, thinking at the same time that billions of people here and why I connected with him only. The thoughts continued and my tears almost faded but what happened next was unbelievable, Rohan hugged me tightly and my tears started rolling up till my cheeks, I can't help myself and continued to cry for a while and he continued to hug me even more tighter now. Maybe I craved for such warmth from decades now and that was the reason my tears were unstoppable. My body felt so numb and brain frozen but my heart just craved for him now. For a moment it felt like I finally got some peace which I craved for many years now.. He was speechless after he heard my story ,he told me not to worry and said he is always with me, he cheered me up with his silly jokes and we headed back towards the car. He drove cheering me up all the way long and dancing his ass off to the beats of some desi music. We made an agreement that we will go for the vacation the next week with all the members of our group. He dropped me to the college gate and I headed towards my car never willing to drive all alone back to basic but the world isn't a wish granting factory as said by John Green, so in real life I need to face all this, drive the car by myself which I found to be a lazy stuff. I just reached the gate and realized he still waited for me to bid good-bye.

I am finally feeling myself again after a long talk with Rohan and remembering what all happened today I was blushing secretly. Indeed was a good day to me! But I promised him about the vacation but my parents won't allow me to. I kept thinking about the excuse I was about to make. It was ten at night, all were in their rooms busy with their own lives unaware of what the other person is doing. The door bell rang and now what? Guests! Holy crap!

I was called downstairs and yes before going I was supposed to change my clothes and do my hair carefully. A second call for me was made and I rushed downstairs. What? Rohan here? How could he be such a jerk he followed me up here? Dammit! All together with his parents. I was left completely blank with thoughts crisscrossing why he showed up here. Suddenly daddy introduced his father as his old friend from the same batch and Rohan told that we were friends too. I had a sigh of relief and internally blushing to see him again. While everyone talked daddy insisted him to come with me up till my room. We walked away and I was completely embarrassed about what to say. Such a moron I'm. to avoid this awkward silence, I asked him if he wish to join for a movie and we grabbed our seats switched on for a movie meanwhile he asked if I was alright now, I simply nodded and said thank you for today and in return I got a beautiful smile from him and that filled me up with positive vibes. I was so happy meeting him again. And it was time for him to leave. we decided to meet tomorrow and discuss for the trip. He knew how my parents were so the time he and his family were leaving he asked if I was joining for the trip and then my mum couldn't deny so I was in for that too now. How he entered my life and all got cheered up. Maybe he was just meant to be with me.

The next day we met and I dressed to impress after all he is the man every other woman looks for. He is worth waiting for, I whispered gently to myself and I got "So are you!" in return from Rohan he heard me whispering.

"Come. Let's have lunch." he said. Searching for Sahil, Tanu and Alisha.

"You look so perfect just don't forget to smile more often!" he made this statement and I'm way too flattered for him now. He wasn't buttering but ya of course that was the truth. Why for god's sake not notice me? Okay so I flaunted more about all this but who cares if it's me or the big knickers I'm wearing. LOL.

My trousers have shrunk so tight around my bottoms that I can't bend my legs. This is hilarious. Ugh! What can I do, what can I do? Brrr. My top is all wet of this snoring heat and sweat. And there are two bumpy things in it. He was so handsome. His hair are all floppy, he had on dark jeans and white t-shirt with dark long eyelashes and a big mouth, sort of soft looking. He's not a girlie boy though, he's definitely a boyie boy, which I think is handy in a boy itself. Hahahahah.

The trip was postponed till further notices and days passed by, we connected more beautifully and life felt like life, I certainly gave up on life but I guess he was my one reason why not too.

I love him, I love him. I love you, Rohan, oh yes I do. When I'm not near you I'm blue… what else rhymes with Rohan? Mohan? I can't sleep, life is too brilliant. I may never sleep again. My days were that fab. He usually played me a song on his guitar. I didn't really know what to do when he does that too me. I decided I am going to be nice to everyone from now on. I will be grown up and nice.

Weeks passed by and I enjoyed everything, parents no more seemed as a torture on my head, my life was running smoothly.

 The next day, he texts me "we need to talk!" what was this all about? Is he going to propose me? Damnn! Yeyee! I got ready and that day I took almost an hour to figure out proper makeup that matches my skin. Dumb creature I'm actually a weird creature you must agree. I drove to college and I was excited and dressed with high heels, proper makeup and dark blue skin tight knee length piece. Hair wide open and a big smile on my face. This morning I was a little late,

and saw Rohan with some other guy. At first I thought this is just normal but the next moment I was shocked seeing the way they became so touchy and the other random guy he was with I guess he is his classmate, kissed Rohan on cheeks, something really unusual. He saw me and they separated, he came closer to me, hugged me in middle of the ground and said "I'm so sorry Saumya, I know I must have told this before to you but I wasn't sure how would you react."

"Okay! What is this all about?" I asked knowing something bad is going to happen.

"I love you, Soumya! But…"

"But.. What Ro?"

"I'm bisexual."

I got numb for few seconds and then realized it's alright I hugged him and said "I love you too Ro, but I'm not into girls."

We laughed and everything went on a perfect note until he forced me to talk to my parents about what all happened to me the other day and all the sufferings I am handling which were useless and worthless. I simply ignored his gestures and this topic every time we met. But managed to love him more every day. So I considered him to be the only reason why not too. But was this uncertain and too early to make this statement?

CHAPTER EIGHT

"Soumya, please explain what's this?" , Mum-ma smashing over that paper on my face.

As I read tears rolled up and the next second I saw myself falling apart I realized Ro wrote this letter. I felt completely numb and cold both at the same time, my mind stopped working. The letter wrote:

Dear Uncle and Aunt,

I'm sorry to say but I just realized your daughter needs you and isn't able to share her views for what she's being punished for and now this has been a while. She suffered mental torture and harassment both at the same time. She never wanted you to bother about but she needs you more than anyone else.

Thank you.

I'm not in the state to explain things to anyone and everything seems to end up so quickly. Sudden thought strikes within, is he breaking up with me sending such letter isn't appreciated I can't believe he did this how from the universe people get so guts in life to hurt the people they love. Was all this love fake? Was I alone suffering with the madness everything kept me busy thinking but how could I not deny to the fact that people do leave, we aren't suppose to expect anything from anyone. And of course endings can't be perfect so as we ain't living in some Disney land.

My parents were angry too they turned red hearing the story I narrated pointing out my mistake so as to not dance or bang onto the floor. I knew this was about to happen but rest was all never imagined.

It has been three months now that I've steeped out of my room my face turned pale surrounding near to death, food almost was served to me in my room everything seems to be ended and how everything wrapped up ending with no conversation even I never bothered to know if he tried contacting me or not I was so lost to myself handling my emotions privately that I am not feeling strong anymore, barely alive!

CHAPTER NINE

This day seems a little different it has been three months and two weeks now, I felt completely under grounded. But today my parents are here with me to talk. What this is all about?

"We are really sorry", Daddy said.

Is someone dead, Granny? The good lady next door, she has been unwell past few years surviving out of cancer stage-3, what was this sorry all about?

Awkward silence followed.

"We know, we ain't good parents but everyone deserves a change in life! Will you?" Mum-ma said.

Oh……ohhhhh. So this is what! I stared at them for two minutes and they hugged me.

You know what I just thought? They literally hugged when I'm eighteen and in past ten years they never hugged me, but today I was feeling on cloud nine. I cried and hugged them back more tightly. And they handed over the phone to me where the recent update in news stated jail for that driver under Article(s) 14, 15, 19(1)(g), 21, 42, 51A, 51 and 253.

This day made my life. I was way too happy, enjoying and celebrating to earn my parents back.

I slept peacefully, Good Night!

CHAPTER TEN

I am the one who has all this. I am different from this. I know that I am this. I am absolutely sure. But, there is only one question that is unanswered- I don't know who I am!

My realization can't be explained completely in a few pages, but for sure I'll make you wonder and ponder about the same question. While we need a body and a soul to realize the truth, I learned that my realization went through two loops of who I am! And who I'm not!

I am not a depressed girl! And, I am a happy-go-lucky charm! Indeed!

Whenever we encounter any different situation be it good or bad, being humans our brains are designed to react to any new change, by analyzing and rationalizing it in such a way that we're influenced with the reasons it provide to support its analysis.

I almost gave up on my life but my one reason why not to was my FAMILY!

CHAPTER ELEVEN

But this wasn't the end, sooner or later I realized that if Rohan would have never wrote that later to my parents, no such incident would have take place and I cannot even expect to get such handful moments and time with my family. I wanted to talk to him again I knew that he never did anything with some wrong intentions. He loved me and why he will hurt me for the way we were happy together, mindful of his bisexuality but its altogether correct it's his own personal choice to stay or leave. If not as lovers why to destroy our friendship man, these thoughts irritated me for a while but then I made up my mind to talk to him the very next day I stepped into the college.

Next day I was lavishly dressed, not sounding depressed anymore and drove to college sounding desperate to see Rohan.

Oh…..oohhh my eyes still can't believe what I saw, he was with his classmate, the same classmate who kissed him on his cheek the other day. It was so surprising. He is Pranav only if I remember his name, Ro's classmate. Rohan was smiling at him patiently while Pranav calmly grabs his hand and places his hand over his cheek. I closed my eyes as they wanted to kiss but I can't just surrender with my feelings for him so easily, I don't know if it was real for

Rohan or not being together but seeing him happy I even felt happier, at least he was happy with what he has now. I wanted to talk to him but decided to talk to him later, thanking him for what all he did. I headed towards the classroom to find Tanu and Alisha. I saw Tanu with Sahil together, Gosh! Why is everyone doing so much lovie dovie everywhere. I started ignoring all the couples around me. I'm hating them now! Even worse happened, I was returning back to my car and saw Alisha and her boyfriend at the college gate. Holy crap! I smashed my foot onto my car and drove aggressively back home. I returned back home realizing good food was being cooked, Mum baked a cake for me and ordered some pizza's. she wanted to talk to me about my current life situations. I was amassed by her gesture but I can't just tell her what all was happening, like what was I supposed to answer? My love life? that I'm in love with a guy wait not guy but my ex who's not into me but is bisexual where my inner self is happy for him accepting him the way he is but anyhow I'm in love with Rohan, I couldn't deny this fact.

She asked me about the trip which was postponed was just next week. We talked about general opinions to bitching for everyone, judging our relatives and spent some good quality time, indeed! It's five in the evening and we decided to go shopping for my trip.

 I'm flattered with this amazing treatment, feels so amazing.

White jeans, blue jeans, shorts, knickers; checked.
Tube tops, crop tops, off shoulder tops, jackets; checked.
Sleeping Pills; checked. These are required as when I run out of anxiety and over thinking.

Toothbrush, Toothpaste, Toothbrush Cover & Dental Floss, Deodorant, sunscreen and aftersun; checked.

Slippers, snickers, heels; checked.

All set for the trip, its already three in the afternoon and I'm supposed to reach the station by four thirty. Jeez help me out! I changed with my comfy clothes for the start of the journey, I bid farewell to my family and daddy dropped me to the station. Everyone is excited about the trip, myself included! Maybe just partially. The group was completely divided into couples and I was the one left out. Tanu and Sahil sat together in the train, Alisha and Dev her boyfriend sat together, it was an unofficial trip so Dev managed to join us for the trip and Rohan and Pranav sat together, it has been a while since I joined the college back and Rohan was completely ignoring me being busy with Pranav every time. I wasn't willing to show that I care too much for Ro till date, the journey started we gossiped for three long hours, the basic humour that was exchanged Sahil always taking the lead and now everyone is busy in their own world of couple goals and fantasies. I decided not to go on with my useless thoughts, took two sleeping pills and slept on the top most birth of the train, the clock said eleven thirty we were told we would reach by six in the morning. I slept peacefully.

The next day we checked into our hotels at one in the afternoon. We are being advised to get freshened up by three.

The day was spent well enjoying to the beats of evergreen nature and beautiful destinations. It is purely a heaven on earth!

Its twelve, midnight and Tanu puffed a cigarette between her lips, lighted it and seems stressful she almost drank half of the bottle of vodka.

"Is everything fine." I asked Tanu. She simply ignored me and nodded after a complete silence. She ordered some raw eggs from the house keeping.

"Okay so what's next, Tanu?" I said and smirks. Sahil and Tanu fought on my useless topic where Sahil was caught red handed flirting with the trip organizer. She called Priyanshi, Khushi, Jyoti, Sanjana, Taruneet and Kiran our friends, sweethearts in general but are partners in crime. We went searching for Sahil with some eggs in our hand, half drunked shouting Sahil's name in whole resort. At the entrance we found a black Audi and therefore Sahil with the trip organizer, making out in the car. Tanu shouted, "you bastard, you cheat! Guys smash these eggs on to them."

We started throwing eggs onto the car, Taruneet slips and bangs on her booty with the egg although she's badly hurt but still continues to smash eggs and we started running away I'm still having the last egg in my hand we are laughing like complete morons, Kiran has now started rolling on the floor laughing so hard, Jyoti banging on the floor with crazy dance moves and Priyanshi still wondering what all we did. Khushi has been a fun loving girl as always gets drunk, she still has her vodka in her hand and is laughing for no reason past ten minutes. Also, Sanjana has been a kid since ever she started crying in the corner for being mean with Sahil for throwing eggs on him, such a jerk. Hahahah! Rohan entering the scene asking us about what we did to Sahil, Tanu snatches away the last egg from me and gives a tight smash on Rohan's face.

To be continued....

www.ingramcontent.com/pod-product-compliance
Lightning Source LLC
LaVergne TN
LVHW050423160726
843469LV00041B/1209